For Tom and Harriet with love PF
For Granny Fair and Nana Smith xx BMS

First published in the UK in 2018 by
Pavilion Books Company Limited
43 Great Ormond Street
London
WC1N 3HZ

Text © Polly Faber, 2018
Illustrations © Briony May Smith, 2018

The moral rights of the author and illustrator have been asserted

Publisher and Editor: Neil Dunnicliffe
Assistant Editor: Harriet Grylls
Art Director: Anna Lubecka

ISBN: 9781843653691

A CIP catalogue record for this book is available from the British Library.

10 9 8 7 6 5 4 3 2 1

Reproduction by Rival Colour Ltd, UK
Printed by Toppan Leefung Printing Ltd, China

This book can be ordered directly from the publisher online at www.pavilionbooks.com,
or try your local bookshop.

Grab That Rabbit!

Grab That Rabbit!

Written by Polly Faber

Illustrated by Briony May Smith

PAVILION

Here's Hodge. Hodge is a white rabbit with one black splodge.
A large white rabbit with one black splodge. Hodge is a happy rabbit, usually.

But today Hodge is a...

…wedged rabbit. An in-the-hedge rabbit.
Hodge was happy. He was happy when he was eating the carrots.

Before he'd tried to wriggle back.
Now Hodge cannot budge. Which also means he cannot dodge…

...Mrs Sprat.
Here's Mrs Sprat, in her large hat,
arriving at her vegetable patch.
Mrs Sprat is usually a happy gardener.

She has come to pull the carrots for her dinner.

There are **no** carrots for her dinner.

Mrs Sprat takes off her hat.

Mrs Sprat spies Hodge: "That rabbit!"

Mrs Sprat rolls up her sleeves.
Her hands reach out.

She pulls, not carrots
but Hodge's bottom.

"Got him!"

POP!

SPLAT!

Mrs Sprat falls
back on *her* bottom.
And on her hat.

"STOP!"

Hop, hop, hop.

Mrs Sprat can't grab that rabbit! Happy Hodge is on the run.

He doesn't see the shape above him...

...a different hazard.

Here, in the sky, is a
large and hungry
buzzard.

The buzzard grabs a good-sized meal. The buzzard is happy.

So long Hodge.
Farewell.
Goodbye.

Still...

...Hodge is wriggling. The buzzard's struggling.
That rabbit's quite a weight to hold...

Hodge d*r*o*p*s*!*

PLOP!

Onto the flat hat of Mrs Sprat. What a relief.
What a happy, happy Hodge! It's just
as well he wasn't thinner.

But...

SCOOP! "Mine!"

Hodge's ears droop.

Mrs Sprat is happy. She's got her catch quite safe this time.
No carrots; perhaps she'll have a rabbit dinner.

Hodge looks up at Mrs Sprat.
He's met his match.
She is the winner.

Mrs Sprat feels Hodge is warm
and squidgy round the tum.
Hodge is a heavy rabbit.
A very soft and fluffy rabbit.

Mrs Sprat sighs.
Does she fancy
rabbit pie?

Here's Hodge,
a white rabbit with
one black splodge.

Here's Mrs Sprat,
back in her squashed hat.

Now Hodge is lodged on
Mrs Sprat's lap. Mrs Sprat
is wedged. She cannot budge.
And *both* of them are...

...happy.